Steve, Terror of the seas

megan Brewis

Kane Miller
A DIVISION OF EDC PUBLISHING

Hi, I'm Steve.

I'm a VERY scary fish.

Small fish are scared of me.

And **BIG** fish are scared of me.

EVERYONE under the sea is afraid.

And as for humans . . .

...they are **terrified!**

I'm not sure what it is that
makes me so scary . . .

I'm not particularly big.

About 12 inches

My teeth aren't too bad . . .

. . . are they?

And though I'm no angelfish . . .

I've seen far *scarier* fish in these waters.
Have a look for yourself . . .

Finding love has been a challenge.

And being scary
can seem like a lonely life.

But you haven't met my best friend, George . . .

THE TRUE PART

The ocean can be a dangerous place for fish, as there are many hungry predators around!

Some fish swim in large groups, called schools or shoals. This gives them the appearance of being larger than they really are, and protects them from bigger fish.

Steve is a pilot fish.

Pilot fish choose a very big scary friend to protect them!

In return for keeping them safe,

pilot fish keep sharks free of harmful parasites.

This friendship is called a mutualistic relationship.

Sharks even allow pilot fish to clean their teeth!

(Pilot fish are not really scary at all!)

Smile, George! Show them your shiny teeth!

For Jackson-M.B.

First American Edition 2019
Kane Miller, A Division of EDC Publishing

Text and illustrations copyright © Megan Brewis 2018

Steve, Terror of the Seas was originally published in English in 2018.
This edition is published by arrangement with Oxford University Press.

For information contact:
Kane Miller, A Division of EDC Publishing
PO Box 470663
Tulsa, OK 74147-0663
www.kanemiller.com
www.edcpub.com
www.usbornebooksandmore.com

Library of Congress Control Number: 2018942386

Printed in China
1 2 3 4 5 6 7 8 9 10

ISBN: 978-1-61067-825-4